Sum

of

Recovery: Freedom from Our Addictions

Russell Brand

Conversation Starters

By BookHabits

Please Note: This is an unofficial conversation starters guide. If you have not yet read the original work or would like to read it again, <u>get the book here.</u>

We hope you enjoy this complementary guide from BookHabits.
Our mission is to aid readers and reading groups with quality, thought provoking material to in the discovery and discussions on some of today's favorite books.

Tips for Using BookHabits Conversation Starters:

EVERY GOOD BOOK CONTAINS A WORLD FAR DEEPER THAN the surface of its pages. The characters and their world come alive through the words on the pages, yet the characters and its world still live on. Questions herein are designed to bring us beneath the surface of the page and invite us into the world that lives on. These questions can be used to:

- Foster a deeper understanding of the book
- Promote an atmosphere of discussion for groups
- Assist in the study of the book, either individually or corporately
- Explore unseen realms of the book as never seen before

About Us:

THROUGH YEARS OF EXPERIENCE AND FIELD EXPERTISE, from newspaper featured book clubs to local library chapters, *BookHabits* can bring your book discussion to life. Host your book party as we discuss some of today's most widely read books.

Table of Contents

Introducing *Recovery:*
Freedom from Our Addictions

Russel Brand is an English comedian and actor whose material regularly covers observational comedy, black comedy, and improvisation. His involvement in comedy, television, film, and activism have made him a prominent public figure since the beginning of his popular career in 2004. "Recovery: Freedom from Our Addictions" is a memoir detailing the author's experiences with mental health issues, specifically focusing on addiction and the process of recovery. Brand's memoir is divided into separate chapters structured around a process of recognizing personal issues and addressing them; his step-by-step explanation encourages readers not only to acknowledge the trouble they are facing but to confide in others and trust in making a change. The structure of the book is meant to help guide the reader through each step that takes one to admitting a problem; while it does promise the possibility and steps for recovery, it is meant more to start the reader on the path to change rather than guide them extensively through the change itself. Brand begins his novel with an introduction detailing the facts surrounding life as he knows it and how it may affect an individual; he speaks about the inevitability of death and how temporary fixes or distractions are often more destructive than helpful when trying to live an even remotely fulfilled life. Brand specifically notes his 'gift of desperation' and how ultimately, his terrible choices and lifestyle forced him to seek and accept help. As the author points out, waiting to become the person you would like or plan to be is in some ways pointless when time is forever marching forward, leaving you with less of it to spend. Accepting and adapting to misery, Brand states, is often near the heart of the true issue of addiction; the compulsion that addiction is fueled by is the need to solve or lessen the pain of disconnection and despair.

Brand's novel begins with a chapter about the Twelve Steps. The famous program, he posits, is actually life-changing when followed thoroughly and with dedication. From the beginning, Brand addresses the wording of the 12 Step program and how the use of God can sometimes push people away; he emphasizes that the core of the program, rather than the words used to detail it, is what is ultimately effective. As Brand points out, saying 'maybe for you, but not for me' is one of the most insidious and self-centered things a person can say. In his experience, even painting oneself as a reluctant or tired caregiver can be self-centered in the way it takes an issue and makes it about you, rather than the person who is truly suffering. The author heavily emphasizes the point that the 12 Steps are neither meant to oppress nor exploit; they are, quite obviously, meant to help. Fighting against the steps, therefore, is not really indicative of an individualistic passion or virtue- it is a mechanism to protect what is often the very self that is destructive and harmful. Throughout the novel, Brand works to emphasize important cycles and warning signs of addiction, including the five-point cycle of pain, temporary distraction, guilt, and a resurgence of pain. Interestingly, much of Brand's argument for recovery and dealing with addiction is, as he points out, connected to very Eastern philosophies; he stresses the importance of creating an immediate change rather than imagining long-term plans. Rather than imagine twenty years of sobriety, the author explains, it is far more helpful to squash the impulse as it comes during any given day, always starting anew and without any excuses for a tiny allowance that might cause one to slip back into bad habit. As the author draws through all of the messy and painful steps of recognizing and beginning to address addiction, he uses his personal battle to inform each of the steps and their efficacy. By the close of the book, Brand lauds the 12-Step program and the way its basic principles helped him recognize his culpability and ability to save himself. Injected with both humor and understanding, Brand's narrative recognizes the fault in every addict and attempts to remind the reader that they can, in fact, change.

A veteran and star in the entertainment industry, Russell Brand continues to develop his tumultuous public image with an apparently new and refreshed take on life and the nature of his addictive personality. "Recovery: Freedom from Our Addictions" recognizes the common issues shared by addicts, allowing readers to relate and learn from the experience of the author. Brand's memoir is a thoughtful and interesting read, offering perspective, advice, and sometimes, humor for anyone struggling with addiction and the path to recovery.

Discussion Questions

"Get Ready to Enter a New World"

Tip: Begin with questions dealing with broader issues to ensure ample time for quality discussions. Read through all discussion questions before engaging.

~~~

question 1

Brand introduces his take on the 12 Steps at the beginning of the book, which serve as chapter headers for different sections of the book. What is your opinion of this organization?

~~~

~~~

question 2

The author seems to recognize his narcissistic personality and how it affected his addiction and life. Do you think he is a credible source, given his past? Why or why not?

~~~

~~~

question 3

In most of the book, the author claims to be self-aware enough to recognize his faults. Do you agree with this characterization? Why or why not?

~~~

~~~

question 4

Most of Brand's narrative points out the issues of modern tools- such as technology- and how they enable and fuel addiction. What is your opinion of his stance? Why?

~~~

~~~

question 5

Many of Brand's issues with addiction come up
when he is a celebrity. Do you feel that he is a
reasonable representation or are his struggles and
experiences singular?

~~~

~~~

question 6

Most of the novel focuses on internal conflict and how to recognize and change it. Do you think there are outside factors Brand ignores or does not sufficiently address? Why or why not?

~~~

~~~

question 7

As you read the novel, are you able to follow the author's logic and beliefs? Why or why not? If there is something you disagree with, why?

~~~

~~~

question 8

Much of what Brand talks about is dissatisfaction and how it fuels addiction. Do you feel that the author's experiences with addiction are genuine? Do you think his story could help someone with addiction? Why or why not?

~~~

~~~

question 9

In some sections, Brand refers to situations that occurred when he was a child or in the past. Do you ever find the narrative confusing? Why or why not?

~~~

~~~

question 10

What do you believe is the most apparent theme in the book, aside from addiction and recovery? Why? Give examples.

~~~

~~~

question 11

Do you find that the author is sufficiently unbiased, or does he make points at any part in the book that seem lacking understanding or perspective? If so, give examples and explain.

~~~

~~~

question 12

Do you think Brand is practical in his advice? Would it be easily implemented by the average reader? Why or why not?

~~~

~~~

question 13

After reading the novel, are you able to gain
perspective you previously did not have? Why or
why not? Do you believe this novel should be read
by others to gain perspective?

~~~

~~~

question 14

Are you able to follow the themes and situations in the book easily? If not, why? Do you think it is reasonable to ask for understanding, or should you not have to do any work?

~~~

~~~

question 15

Addiction, recovery, and the process from within are all heavily discussed in Brand's book. Do you think the book is written well to make these topics relatable? Why or why not?

~~~

~~~

question 16

"Recovery: Freedom from Our Addictions" is not the author's first book. Do you anticipate it making a bestseller list or not? Why? If so, what list?

~~~

~~~

question 17

This novel focuses on addiction, recovery, and changing one's life. Do you think this book fits the author's themes? Why or why not? Does it seem common at all, or is it a new approach to the subject?

~~~

question 18

Most of the novel relies on personal experience and popular methods of implementing change and recovery. Do you think these makes the novel more reliable? Why or why not?

~~~

question 19

Brand's experience with addiction pushed him to make a change. Do you think that he is understanding of the difference between different types of addicts, or is there any point at which he seems too invested in his personal journey?

~~~

~~~

question 20

The book is a memoir, relying on the author's memory and retelling of his experiences. Do you think this was a good choice for the novel? Why or why not?

~~~

Introducing the Author

Russell Brand was born June 4, 1975 in Grays, Essex, England. He was the only child of Barbara Elizabeth and Ronald Henry Brand, a photographer. Brand's parents separated when he was six months old and he lived with his mother; he had a difficult childhood and was sexually abused by a tutor at the age of seven. Brand's mother contracted uterine cancer when he was eight years old, then contracting breast cancer one year later; Brand lived with relatives during her treatment. At fourteen, Brand suffered from bulimia and at sixteen, he left home due to disagreements with his mother's partner. At this point, he began using illegal drugs such as LSD and ecstasy. Brand's relationship with his father was unconventional; he has mentioned only seeing him sporadically and being taken to Thailand to visit prostitutes as a teenager. At fifteen, Brand had debuted in a school theatre production of *Bugsy Malone*, further working as a film extra. In 1991, brand attended Grays School Media Arts College and was accepted into Italia Conti Academy; his first year of tuition was funded by Essex County Council but he was expelled after his first year for illegal drug use and poor attendance.

In 2000, Brand performed stand-up at the Hackney Empire New Act of the Year; while he placed fourth, his performance attracted the attention of Nigel Klarfeld, agent for *Bound and Gagged Comedy Ltd.* Brand continued to work as a comedian, eventually launching a nationwide tour in 2006 titled *Shame*. In 2007, Brand co-hosted Teenager Canger Trust evening with Noel Fielding; he laos performed for Queen Elizabeth II and Prince Philip in the Royal Variety Performance. Brand also began performing in the US, recording a special for Comedy Central and also starting a new tour. In October 2009, Brand added dates to his tour to raise money for Focus 12, a drug charity. In 2013, Brand presented and toured a new show; in January 2017, he announced a new who debuting in April and running to November 2018. Aside from stand-up comedy, Brand also presented as a video journalist for MTV and a host for E4's *Big Brother's Eforum*. Brand also presented the 2006 NME Awards and hosted the 2007 BRIT Awards. His roles as an actor have included parts in movies such as *Forgetting Sarah Marshall*, which helped him achieve fame in America; he also starred in the 2010 version of *The Tempest, Rock of Ages*, and *St. Trinian's*. Brand's career has been marked by controversy and wild coverage by tabloids and mainstream media alike. His recent novel, however, seems to mark a change in attitude and perhaps behavior.

Brand published "Recovery: Freedom from Our Addictions" in October 2017. His continued presence in the comedic, film and television spheres have made him a prominent figure with several credits to his name. The author's use of comedy to soften the harsh realities of addiction and recovery continues to appear in his stand-up routines and writing. Brand's novel, which reflects on his past experiences and constant desire to reshape his life, is meant to give readers perspective and direction when facing addiction and recovery. Many readers who enjoy Brand's trademark drama and unabashed tone eagerly await more work from the author, citing his use of unafraid language and realistic struggles as proof of his strength as an author and comedian.

Fireside Questions

"What would you do?"

Tip: These questions can be a fun exercise as it spurs creativity among the readers by allowing alternate scene endings and "if this was you" questions.

~~~

question 21

Brand has worked in film and television, although his primary focus is stand-up comedy. Do you think this is clear in his writing? Why or why not?

~~~

~~~

question 22

The author experienced a fractured and troubled family dynamic from an early age. Do you think this has affected his humor or material? How so? Does it make him more or less relatable as an author?

~~~

~~~

question 23

Much of Brand's publicity has been negative. Many new sources tended to focus on his addictions and perceived bad behavior. Do you think the author has changed at all? Why or why not?

~~~

~~~

question 24

Most of Brand's novel focuses on using his experience to give others advice. Do you agree with his approach? Why or why not?

~~~

~~~

question 25

"Recovery" deals with themes of addiction and other mental health issues. Do you think the author is a reliable authority on the topic? Why or why not?

~~~

~~~

question 26

Brand separates the book by chapters based on his take on the 12 Step program. Do you agree with this method? Why or why not? How would you structure the book?

~~~

~~~

question 27

If you were writing about this topic, would you
have chosen memoir, nonfiction, or fiction? Why?
Does Brand's choice in genre work?

~~~

~~~

question 28

Does the author use sufficient evidence to support his argument? Does it matter? Why?

~~~

~~~

question 29

Brand talks at length about his experience with addiction and treatment. Do you agree with his recounting? Would you have done the same, or would you have avoided giving personal information? Why?

~~~

~~~

question 30

At the beginning of the book, the author quickly sets a specific tone. What do you think it is? Would you have chosen a different tone? Why or why not?

~~~

Quiz Questions

"Ready to Announce the Winners?"

Tip: Create a leaderboard and track scores to see who gets the most correct answers. Winners required. Prizes optional.

quiz question 1

"Recovery: Freedom from Our Addictions"
discusses the use of the
_____. The author stresses
that it is vital to recovery, despite some
representations of it being faith-based.

quiz question 2

Brand points out that addictions stem from
_____; in his explanation,
seeking respite or relief and experiencing guilt feed
into the cycle.

~~~

quiz question 3

At the beginning of the book, Brand references the harm that _____ may do to people suffering from addiction. In his view, it only helps distract people from reality and helps them avoid change.

~~~

~~~

quiz question 4

True or False: The novel is based entirely on
Brand's experiences. Most of what he talks about is
exclusive to his experience as a celebrity but he
attempts to make it relatable.

~~~

~~~

quiz question 5

True or False: "Recovery" is structured in a way that helps people identify, cure, and stay sober. It is meant as a step-by-step guide for addicts that has resources for reference.

~~~

~~~

quiz question 6

True or False: The novel focuses on healing from within, using self-reflection and recognition of personal failings to effect change.

~~~

~~~

quiz question 7

True or False: One of the major themes in the novel is medical incompetency; the author speaks at length about how addiction is entirely spiritual and no outside interference or help should be sought.

~~~

~ ~ ~

quiz question 8

Brand attended Italia Conti Academy but was
expelled for _____. He had
his first year of tuition paid but could not
overcome his addictions.

~ ~ ~

quiz question 9

Brand's career has spanned over three particular mediums: _____. He gained fame in his home country before breaking out in America for his work on MTV.

quiz question 10

Brand's philosophy focuses on recovery as
_____ rather than
planning for twenty years. This 'Eastern
philosophy', the author argues, is easier to enact.

~~~

quiz question 11

True or False:: Brand's parents divorced when he was extremely young; his mother was ill when he was a child and he had a strange relationship with his father.

~~~

~~~

quiz question 12

True or False: Many of Brand's comedy routines involve themes of addiction and mental health issues, which also appear in his writing. He speaks at length about how these struggles have impacted his life.

~~~

Quiz Answers

1.   12 Step program
2.   Lack of fulfilment/unhappiness
3.   technology
4.   True
5.   False
6.   True
7.   False
8.   Drug use, truancy
9.   Television, film, stand-up
10. Day by day
11. True
12. True

Ways to Continue Your Reading

EVERY month, our team runs through a wide selection of books to pick the best titles for readers and reading groups, and promotes these titles to our thousands of readers – sometimes with free downloads, sale dates, and additional brochures.

If you have not yet read the original work or would like to read it again, <u>get the book here.</u>

Want to register yourself or a book group? It's free and takes 1-click.

Register here.

On the Next Page…

Please write us your reviews! Any length would be fine but we'd appreciate hearing you more! We'd be SO grateful.

Till next time,

BookHabits

"Loving Books is Actually a Habit"

CPSIA information can be obtained
at www.ICGtesting.com
Printed in the USA •
LVHW040621061218
599451LV00001B/175/P

9 781389 483806